ZIPPY AND HIS SUPER HERO

Written by Nathan and
Keven McTaggart

Illustrated by Aspenwood
Elementary School
2017/18 Division 2

Zippy and His Super Hero
Copyright © 2018 by Nathan's Super Heroes Book Series
www.NathansSuperHeroes.com

ISBN 978-0-2288-0124-5 (Paperback)

Books by
Nathan and Keven McTaggart

Net Proceeds Donated To the
BC Burn Fund

Net Proceeds Donated to the
Canucks for Kids Fund

Net proceeds of the sale of this book will be
donated to the Canucks for Kids Fund

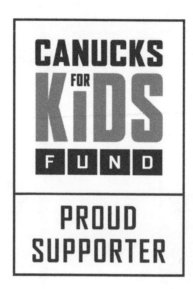

This book is dedicated to Daniel and Henrik Sedin. After 17 years with
the Vancouver Canucks, Daniel and Henrik have hung up their skates.
You were my first hockey heroes and will forever be an inspiration.

Nathan McTaggart

Dear Zippy

When I was 3 years old, my Daddy and I came up with the story of Santa and His Super Hero. Many years later, when I was 8 years old, we decided to turn our story into a book.

When my class was drawing the pictures for Santa and His Super Hero, I started thinking about the year that you were my shelf elf and a dream I had about you introducing me to Santa up at the North Pole.

This story is about the Christmas that we became friends and the adventures we had in my dream.

Nathan

Up at the North Pole, all of the elves were busy making presents. Christmas was just a few hours away and everyone was getting very excited.

Ella

But not all of elves worked at the North Pole. Some of the younger elves were sent around the world to stay with children. They watched over them during the Christmas season and reported back to Santa. You see, Santa is far too busy to be everywhere all of the time so he cleverly recruited Shelf Elves to help him out.

Over at Nathan's house, Zippy the Shelf Elf was getting ready to head back to the North Pole to report to Santa. Nathan was all tucked in for the night and Zippy really wanted to make sure that Nathan stayed on Santa's "Nice List".

As Zippy returned to the North Pole, he didn't realize that he had been followed.

"Zippy, who is that behind you?" asked Santa. Zippy looked back and was startled at what he saw.

"This is young Nathan," said Zippy. "He is a fine little boy... that I thought was sleeping," he added.

"It's great to meet you Santa," Nathan said timidly as he peeked around Zippy.

Santa welcomed him to the North Pole and they shared a plate of Mrs. Claus' Cookies. "These are great cookies," said Nathan. "The best I have ever eaten."

"Nathan," said Santa, "What do you want to be when you grow up?"

Nathan replied without a thought. "A Super Hero!"

"A Super Hero?" inquired Santa.

"Well, I'd like to be a fire fighter, but I'm afraid of heights," explained Nathan, "but all first responders are my Super Heroes."

"That's what I thought," said Santa. Nathan was wearing yellow flannel pajamas that looked like a fire fighter's turnout gear and black winter boots.

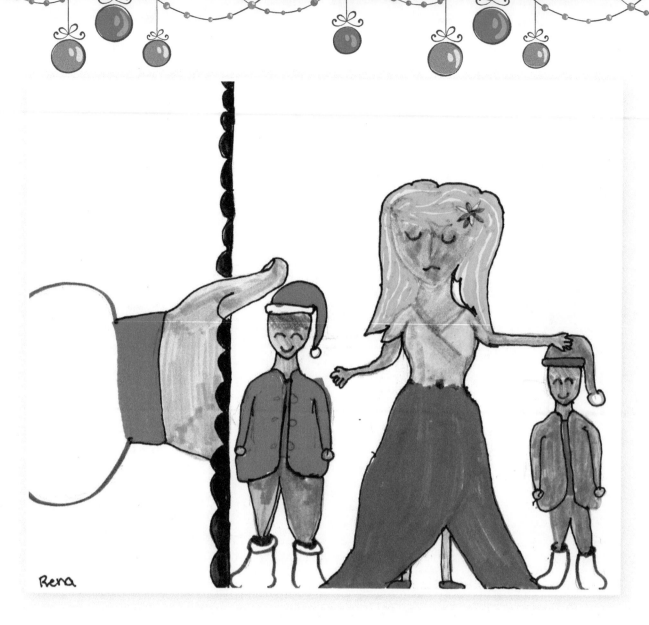

After a few minutes, Nathan asked, "Hey Santa, do you have any brothers or sisters?"

Nathan was very curious.

"Yes, I have a brother and his name is Nick," said Santa. "He lives in the South Pole. I sure wish he could come for a visit. I miss him terribly."

"Why do you live so far apart?" Nathan asked.

"A long time ago, Mother Nature had two boys. I am her oldest son, and Nick is my younger brother," Santa explained.

"We were the best of friends, as brothers should be, until one winter night our mother said to us, 'I love this time of the year. Santa, being my oldest son, I want you to create a new holiday and call it Christmas,' I was so excited."

Seeing that talking about this was making Santa upset, Zippy jumped in. "His brother, Nick, wanted to have a holiday too. The fact that Nick didn't get a holiday made him feel sad and angry. Nick started to do things to disrupt Christmas. Mother Nature wasn't pleased about this, so she divided the Earth in half at the equator and gave the North Pole to Santa and the South Pole to Nick."

"Santa was allowed to go all around the world on Christmas Eve so he could deliver presents to all the children on Earth." Zippy continued.

This reminded Nathan of his cousins who lived far away who he missed terribly. "If there was only a way to reunite Santa with his brother," Nathan thought to himself.

Nathan and Zippy looked at each other and Zippy said, "Are you thinking what I'm thinking?"

"If you're thinking we should go find Nick," said Nathan, "You can count me in."

Zippy borrowed Santa's most reliable sled, harnessed up the reindeer and off they flew. They were at the South Pole in no time.

"Now that we're here," said Nathan, "how do we find Nick?"

"If he is anything like his brother, we'd be able to hear his elves singing for miles," said Zippy. But there was no singing to be heard. Unlike Santa, Nick only had a few elves and they weren't very loud.

"I know…" said Nathan. "Santa has reindeer. I bet Nick has some reindeer too. Let's just look for reindeer tracks and we'll be sure to find him," but reindeer only live in the north. There are no reindeer at the South Pole.

Just then they saw three emperor penguins in the distance. Nathan called out "Hello, lo, lo, lo, lo. Over here, ere, ere, ere, ere," the echoes cried out. The three penguins waddled over to Nathan and Zippy.

They were very proud penguins. The two taller penguins had white bellies, yellow necks and black heads. And they looked like they were going somewhere fancy because they were wearing tuxedos. The smaller one had a black head and white face and she was wearing her fluffy grey pajamas.

"Hi, I'm Nathan and this is Zippy."

"I'm Patty," said the largest penguin in a majestic voice. "And this is my sister Penny and my daughter Pawsie."

"We're looking for a man," said Zippy. "He might be wearing a blue suit and have some elves with him."

"You must be talking about jolly old St. Nick," said Penny. "He lives just over that hill. We can take you to him."

As they reached the top of the hill and looked over to the other side, Nathan couldn't believe his eyes! There he saw a castle made entirely of ice and snow. In front of the castle was one tall evergreen tree. This was the only tree they'd seen the whole time they were at the South Pole. You see, it's too cold, dark and windy for trees to grow in the South Pole, but this was a magical Christmas tree.

Both the castle and the tree were sparkling with beautiful lights of every colour. It looked exactly like where Santa lived, but much smaller.

As they approached Nick's home they saw him with his elves. The elves were trying to make a replica of Santa's sleigh.

"What are you making?" asked Nathan as he walked up behind Nick.

Nick was startled. This was the first time he heard a child's voice in years. "Who are you and what are you doing here?"

"I'm Nathan and this is my Shelf Elf, Zippy. We came down here to find you. We want to know if you would like to come back to the North Pole. Santa really misses you."

"I really miss everyone too," replied Nick. "I have been working on my own sleigh so that I could go back for a visit, but I can't seem to get it to fly."

Nick explained to them how every Christmas Eve, he would decorate his home and his lone tree in hopes that Santa would see it and come for a visit. But deep down inside, he knew that since there was no children anywhere near the South Pole, there was no chance that Santa would see it.

Clare

Looking over at Nick's sleigh, Zippy said, "That is a beautiful sleigh. However, I think I know why it won't fly. You need some magic dust and a few flying reindeer."

Zippy pulled out a bag of magic dust from his jacket and sprinkled it over the sleigh. Instantly, it seemed to come to life. Then he harnessed half of Santa's reindeer to Nick's sleigh. After they loaded his belongings and elves into the two sleighs, Nick said goodbye to Patty, Penny and Pawsie. With a tear running down his cheek, Nick took one last look at his home away from home, and off they flew.

When they got back to the North Pole, Nick's face lit up with joy. He was very happy to be back home where he belonged. After looking around for a couple minutes, they found Santa and Mrs. Claus enjoying their Christmas Eve dinner in the main dining room with all of the elves. "Zippy, you're late for dinner!" bellowed Santa.

"I'm sorry," said Zippy. "Nathan and I were out getting you a very special Christmas present." He pointed over to the door and in walked Nathan and Santa's brother, Nick.

By; Veronika

Santa was overwhelmed with joy, seeing his younger brother after all these years. After a very long hug, Santa invited Nick to join them for dinner before they went on their Christmas Eve travels. Nick pulled up a seat beside Santa at the head table while Zippy and Nathan joined the rest of the elves in the main dining room.

by: Zoey

As dinner came to a close, Santa stood up to make his annual Christmas Eve speech. "I'd like to thank you for all of your hard work this year. This is going to be a very special Christmas."

"I'd like to thank Nathan for following Zippy back to the North Pole," Santa paused. "But don't let it happen again or you might just find yourself on the Naughty List," Santa said with a chuckle.

"I'd really like to thank Nathan and his Shelf Elf, Zippy, for traveling down to the South Pole to find my little brother, Nick," Santa continued. "Zippy, you can continue being Nathan's Shelf Elf for as long as he needs you, as you do such a great job at that, but for the rest of the year, I would like to make you my NEW Head Elf in Training."

Alice and Nathalie

"And finally," Santa declared proudly, "Nick has agreed to help me on my Christmas Eve run this year."

The room erupted with cheers as Santa and Nick left the dining room, followed closely by Nathan and Santa's NEW Head Elf in Training, Zippy.

They loaded into Santa's sleigh. Santa in his best red Christmas suit, Nick in his bright blue suit, Zippy in his new green Head Elf in Training uniform, and Nathan in his yellow flannel pajamas.

As they made their rounds, Nick was surprised with a little detour to the South Pole where Santa had a special delivery of Antarctic Krill for Nick's penguin pals, Patty, Penny and Pawsie.

When they reached Nathan's house, Nick and Zippy joined Santa as they took Nathan back to his room. While Santa was placing the presents under the Christmas tree, Nick and Zippy said their goodbyes.

"Thank you for finding me at the South Pole and for all your help," said Nick. "This is the best Christmas present ever."

Vanessa

"Work hard and you will be able to achieve anything," Zippy said softly as he tucked Nathan in. "I bet you could even become a fire fighter if you want it badly enough. With your help, we were able to reunite Santa with his brother and made this the best Christmas ever. You truly are my Super Hero."

Just then Santa entered the room and knelt beside Nathan's bed. "You had quite a night young man," whispered Santa. "You will go to sleep now and when you wake up, this evening's adventures will be just a dream. I have a feeling, however, when you grow up, you and Zippy will do some great things together."

With that, Santa stood up, pulled a bag of magic dust from his jacket and sprinkled a bit of it over Nathan's head and off to sleep he went.

When Nathan woke up Christmas morning, he saw, on his dresser, a large snow globe. In the snow globe there was a sleigh with an elf, a fire fighter and two Santa's. One was wearing red and one was wearing blue. And they were flying over a field of snow with three penguins looking up.

same.

Nathan took his new snow globe into his parent's room, sat on the foot of their bed and started telling them about his best Christmas adventure EVER!

ABOUT THE BOOK

When Nathan was in grade 4, his class did the illustrations for our first book, Santa and His Super Hero. What we didn't know was that his teacher, Mrs. Shinkewski had her class illustrate our book to teach them about the process of creating a story.

That Christmas, Nathan wrote the story of Zippy and His Super Hero. When we read the story, we instantly fell in love with the characters and the story that Nathan created.

Over the next 2 years, Nathan and I worked on expanding the story and developing the characters in this book.

ABOUT THE CANUCKS FOR KIDS FUND

One of the things that Nathan is passionate about is helping his community. We will be donating part proceeds from every book that we sell to a charity associated with the Super Hero in our books.

Another thing Nathan is passionate about is hockey. Since there are no First Responders in this book, we decided to give to the Canucks for Kids Fund.

The Canucks for Kids Fund dedicates resources to assist charities which support children's health and wellness, foster the development of grassroots hockey, and facilitate and encourage education in British Columbia.

ABOUT THE AUTHORS

This is the second book for Nathan and Keven McTaggart. They came up with the story of Santa and His Super Hero when Nathan was just 3 years old.

Since they started the process of publishing their book, they have had an amazing time promoting the book thru the media and visiting many fire halls.

Seeing as Nathan wants to be a First Responder when he gets older, they decided that they will publish a series of Super Hero books about the different First Responders.

ABOUT THE ILLUSTRATORS

Division 2, at Aspenwood Elementary was very excited when they were asked by Nathan to contribute Illustrations for this newest story, "Zippy and His Super Hero". Division 2 is a class of avid and enthusiastic artist who were so pleased to be a part of Nathan's continued mission to support the tireless emergency responders in our community.

The cover was illustrated by Camryn Thind. Camryn is in Grade 6 at Scott Creek Middle School and is a big fan of Nathan's Super Hero Book Series.

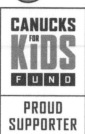

OUR SUPER HEROES

All First Responders are our Super Heroes

....

....

....

....

....

....

....

....

....

....

....

....

....

WE THANK YOU

Have your Super Heroes sign your book

....

....

....

....

....

....

....

....

....

....

....

....

....

AUTOGRAPHS

AUTOGRAPHS

AUTOGRAPHS

This book would not have been possible
without the generosity of our backers

Net proceeds of the sale of this book will be
donated to the Canucks for Kids Fund.

CANUCKS
FOR
KiDS
F U N D

PROUD
SUPPORTER

CPSIA information can be obtained
at www.ICGtesting.com
Printed in the USA
LVHW07s2159080918
589519LV00006B/8/P